Walt Disney's
Pooh's Schoolhouse

Golden Press • New York

Western Publishing Company, Inc.
Racine, Wisconsin

Quick, finish your breakfast. It's almost time for school.

Hurry up or you'll miss the school bus!

On the way, it's fun
to sing "The School Song."

THE SCHOOL SONG
We can't wait till we get to school...
To read and write and count and sing...
To work and play and learn and fool...
And hear the 12 noon lunch bell ring.

Try not to be late. (Sometimes it's hard not to be
late when you're carrying something heavy.)

When you get to school, hang up your coats
and jackets and sweaters and scarves and hats
and mittens and umbrellas and boots. (If you
don't have anything to hang up, you can pretend.)

Then you can put away your lunch until lunchtime. Who has the biggest lunch? Who has the smallest lunch? Who has the medium-sized lunch?

Ring! There's the bell. As soon as the bell rings,
sit down at your desk. Who is sitting down? Who is
standing up? (Isn't it funny someone can't spell "honey"?)

A wonderful way to start each day is to listen to others, and enjoy what they would like to share with you. People enjoy telling about lots of things—places they have visited, things they have done, their hobbies, and anything at all. Have you ever heard anyone show something and tell about it? What have you heard? Do you have anything you want to show and tell?

Of course, there are always some people who want to do all the talking and never want to listen to anyone else. Then there are other people who are so busy thinking of what they are going to say when it's their turn, that they don't hear anything, either. And there are some people who don't want to show, tell, or listen—they are more interested in other things.

SUN   RAIN   SNOW

After show and tell, there's probably not too much left to talk about except the weather. It's always good to be able to talk about the weather if you are at a party and can't think of anything else to say. Of course, not everyone cares about the weather, but in case you do, can you tell who is dressed for winter? Who is dressed for rain? Who looks like he is going to swim? Who is dressed for snow?

15

After you have talked about the
weather, maybe it would be good to learn
how to read. Most people who can read
know the letters in the alphabet. Can you
name all the letters?

Blackboard

$1 + 0 = 1$

Zero

Map

Violin

Eraser   Chalk

Globe

Orange

Indian hat

Xylophone

Honey jar

HUNNY

Ruler

Desk

Umbrella

Quilt

Yo-yo

Very good! Now that you have worked so hard, how about having a parade to celebrate? A parade is lots of fun, and one of the best kinds is one where you wear different hats. What do you want to be? A firefighter? An Indian chief? A clown? A witch? A king?

A parade is even better with music! Pick out an instrument to play, or just pretend. Boom! Bang! Squeak! Crash! Boing!

PARADE

21

When parade time is over, put away your
instruments and hang up your hat on the hat rack.
The pictures and words on each sign show you
where to put each hat. Are all the hats in the right
places? Which hats are in the wrong places?

MAGICIAN

WITCH

COOK

PIRATE

INDIAN CHIEF

BAND LEADER

CLOWN

FIREMAN

After all that marching, let's play "Detective."
To play "Detective," first you figure out who is
holding what shape. Who is holding the circle? Who
is holding the square? Who has the triangle? What is
the name of the shape that looks like a long, skinny
square? If you know all the answers, you're a pretty
good detective.

Now comes the exciting part! The teacher
puts all the shapes on a table. Take a good look,
because in a minute some shapes are going to
disappear.

Hide your eyes, and no peeking, please. When you open your eyes, a shape will be missing. If you had five shapes and one is gone, how many will be left?

A. How many shapes are left?

C. What shape is on the table?

B. What is missing? Can you name the shapes that are left?

D. What is missing? How many objects are left?

After you have played "Detective," maybe you'd like to listen to all the different sounds in the room, or you can make your own sound. A POP might mean someone's bubble gum has broken. A TRALAA might be someone singing. A SHHHH might mean someone is trying to make you be quiet. You also might BARK like a dog, SQUEAK like a chalk, or WHISTLE like the wind. What other sounds can you make?

25

GROWL! What's *that* sound? A lion? A bear?
Nope, it's somebody's tummy growling. You can tell
that it's almost time to eat when you hear that
noise. The lunch bell is going to ring soon. Should
everybody jump up and run and grab the food when
they hear the bell, or is there another way to get
lunch? If you guessed, "Make a line and wait your
turn," you were right. But who will be first in line?

12 INCHES = 1 FOOT

One good way to see who will be first is to line up by size. But how do you know who is what size? One way to find out is to measure each other. The shortest people will stand in the front part of the line and the tallest people will stand at the end of the line.

This looks like a pretty good line. Who is the tallest? Who is the shortest? Who is in the wrong place? Where do you think he should be?

Lunch at last! There are a few things you should and shouldn't do when you are eating. Can you see things that people are doing that really shouldn't be done? Is *anybody* doing *anything* right?

Yummy! That was delicious! But look at the table and the chairs and the floor! Is this a nice way to leave the table? What could you do to make it look better?

After lunch, it's time to take a short rest and let
your food digest before you get back to work. Who
do you think is on the red blanket? Who has a
purple blanket? Where is the green blanket?
Who has a yellow blanket? Who is lying on the
blue blanket?

While you are resting, try to take a nap. One way
to get to sleep is to close your eyes and try to picture
your favorite things. Then try to count them. This is
one reason why it's useful to know how to count.
Can you guess whose dreams these are?

Ring! There goes the alarm clock. Time to get up. Hurry!

When rest is over, you're probably full of energy. Exercise keeps you in shape, and it's fun! It feels good to try to touch your toes without bending your knees. Or you can do ten "jumping jacks." Some people like to run as fast as they can without going anywhere. Or lie on the floor, have a partner hold your feet, and try to sit up.

Some people S-T-R-E-T-C-H instead of
jumping around. You can stand on your toes and
reach for the sky, or for whatever you want!

It's always helpful to know how to count. That way you can be sure you will get as many as you're supposed to. Can you count the things in each picture?

How many tails?

How many feet?

How many rows of carrots? (Somebody made a spelling mistake!)

KERIT KERIT KERIT KERIT KERIT

Count the umbrellas.

How many teapots?

Count the kangaroos.

How many jars of honey?

Count the pine trees.

How many lunches?

How many scarves?

After all that counting, maybe you're ready to sing.
The singing teacher is here to teach you "The Honey Song."

The Honey Song

Seven drops of honey	Six drops of honey
Floating in a pot.	Floating in a pot.
Take away one,	Take away one,
And what have you got?	And what have you got?

Join hands and walk around in a circle while you're
singing. Whenever you sing the words, "Take away
one," somebody should leave the circle, until no one
is left.

Gosh, time goes fast when you're having fun!
It's almost time to go home! But first you'd better
clean up, so that you will come back to a nice clean
room the next time you come to school. What can
you do to help clean up?

When you think the room is in tip-top shape, get your coats and lunch boxes. Maybe your teacher will let you play a game while you are waiting for the bell.

Most people like to play "Follow the Leader."
To play, you just do the same thing the leader
does. Of course, some people *never* do what
everyone else is doing!

RING! There's the bell. My, the day went
fast. And you did so many things. When you get
home and someone asks you what you did in
school today, what will you say?

The day was too short! But tomorrow is
a brand new day!